The Clever Jackals

Retold by Beverley Randell
from an Indian Folk Tale

Illustrations by Pat Reynolds

Rigby

A Harcourt Achieve Imprint

www.Rigby.com
1-800-531-5015

Two little jackals

lived in a green jungle.

Some deer lived there, too.
Every day they all went
down to the river to drink.

One day
a lion came along.
He looked down
at the deer and the jackals.

"I am King of the Jungle!"
he roared.
"I am very hungry.
Come to my cave
so that I can eat you up."

"What can we do?"
cried the deer.
"We don't want the lion
to eat us up!"

"Hide behind the trees,"
said the jackals.
"We will trick the lion.
We won't let him eat
any of us."

The jackals ran to the cave.
"You are **late**!"
roared the lion.

"We are sorry,"
called the jackals.
"We were on our way,
but a bigger lion
tried to stop us.
He said that **he** was
King of the Jungle!"

"He is **not**!" roared the lion.
"I am King of the Jungle!
Take me to him."

The little jackals took the
lion to an old round well.
"The lion lives down there,"
they said.

The lion looked down
inside the well.

He did see a lion . . .
but he was looking
at **himself**
in the water!

"I am King of the Jungle!"
roared the lion.
"I'm coming
to get you!"

The lion jumped down
into the well, and
that was the end of him!

"Clever little jackals!"

said the deer.

"You saved us all."